From the Library of

Beth
Walima

For Strawberry Jam or Fireflies

by Gail Hartman
illustrated by Ellen Weiss

BRADBURY PRESS / NEW YORK

Text copyright © 1989 by Gail Hartman

Illustrations copyright © 1989 by Ellen Weiss

Bradbury Press
An Affiliate of Macmillan, Inc.
866 Third Avenue, New York, NY 10022
Collier Macmillan Canada, Inc.

The text of this book is set in ITC Zapf International Light.
The illustrations are rendered in watercolor and colored pencil.

Printed and bound in Singapore

First American Edition

10 9 8 7 6 5 4 3 2 1

Library of Congress Cataloging-in-Publication Data

Hartman, Gail.   For strawberry jam or fireflies.   Summary: Relates to the uses of such things as a truck tire, a ball of string, a mason jar, and an orange carrot.
[1. Vocabulary]   I. Weiss, Ellen, ill.   II. Title.   PZ7.H26733Fo   1989   [E]   88-30509
ISBN 0-02-742990-3

A BIG TIRE

for rolling down the road

or swinging from a tree

A BALL OF STRING

for a neatly
tied package

or a spider's web

A WOODEN SPOON

for mixing cookies

or tapping a tune

A CARDBOARD BOX

for moving out

or moving in

A PATCHWORK QUILT

for keeping warm

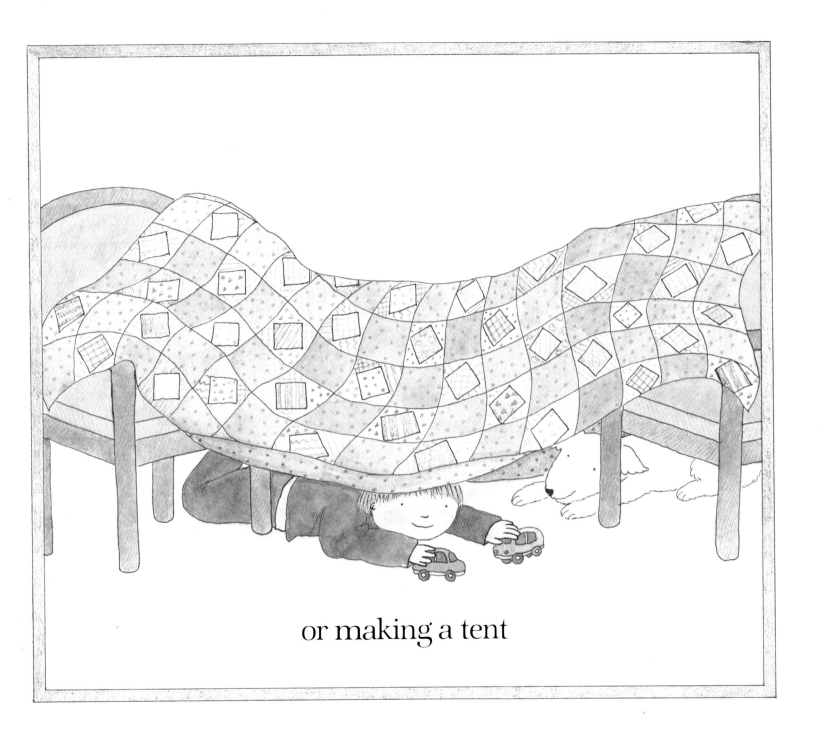

or making a tent

A MASON JAR

for strawberry jam

or fireflies

CHEWY RAISINS

for an afternoon snack

or a funny face on a cookie

A PAPER BAG

for groceries

or a Halloween mask

A DRESSER DRAWER

for folded clothes

or a nice warm bed

AN ORANGE CARROT

for a rabbit's lunch

or a snowman's nose

A PORCH SWING

for a quiet time

or laughing
with a friend